Experiment with a Plant's Roots

Nadia Higgins

Lerner Publications
Minneapolis

Lerner Publications Company
A division of Lerner Publishing Group, Inc.
241 First Avenue North
Minneapolis, MN 55401 USA

For reading levels and more information, look up this title at www.lernerbooks.com.

Library of Congress Cataloging-in-Publication Data

Higgins, Nadia.
    Experiment with a plant's roots / by Nadia Higgins.
        pages cm. — (Lightning bolt books™ Plant experiments)
    Includes index.
    ISBN 978-1-4677-5729-4 (lib. bdg. : alk. paper)
    ISBN 978-1-4677-6243-4 (eBook)
    1. Roots (Botany)—Juvenile literature. 2. Plants—Experiments—Juvenile literature. I. Title.
    II. Series: Lightning bolt books. Plant experiments.
    QK644.H59 2015
    581.4'98—dc23   2014017738

Manufactured in the United States of America
1 – BP – 12/31/14

Table of Contents

How Much of a Plant is Roots?

A giant oak tree's branches stretch into the sky. But did you know you are seeing only part of the tree? Underground, the oak's roots may spread even farther than the branches.

An oak tree can have many branches. But it also has many roots buried underground.

Roots are an important plant part. They take in water and minerals from the soil. They hold the plant in the ground. Roots also store food for the plant.

A dandelion has a long, thick root.

An oak tree's root system is very big. But how much of a backyard weed do you think is hidden in the soil? Make a prediction.

Now let's experiment to find out if you were right!

Trees have lots of roots that spread out.

What you need:

scissors

pencil and paper

shovel

ruler

two different weeds (crabgrass and dandelions work well)

Crabgrass and dandelions are good weeds for this experiment. Ask an adult to help you find weeds that are safe to dig up.

Steps:

1. With an adult's help, dig up two different weeds.

2. Shake off all the dirt from the roots. Rinse the roots with water if you need to.

3. Cut the roots off the weeds.

4. Measure the length of the roots.
   Now measure the top
   of each plant.
   Record your
   results.

Is the root or the top
of this dandelion longer?

Now put your results in a chart. Was your prediction correct?

	Weed 1 (Dandelion)		Weed 2 (Crabgrass)	
	Top	Root	Top	Root
Length				

Your chart should list the lengths of the plant tops and plant roots.

Think It Through

Are the weed tops or the roots longer? Are you surprised by how much of a plant is underground?

How Much Water Do Onion Roots Take Up?

A gardener waters the soil under a plant, not the leaves. Why? It's because the plant's roots take in the water. The roots send water up through the rest of the plant.

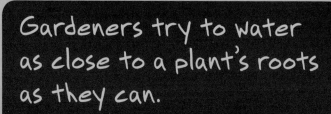

Gardeners try to water as close to a plant's roots as they can.

But just how much water can roots take in? Let's experiment with an onion bulb to find out.

What you need:

liquid plant food

clear jar

plastic cling wrap

water

pencil and paper

onion bulb from a garden store

rubber band

ruler

toothpicks

permanent marker

Steps:

1. Fill the jar with water and add a few drops of plant food.

2. Push the toothpicks into the onion. Use them to balance the onion on the rim of the jar. Make sure the bottom of the onion touches the water.

Mark the water level on the outside of the jar using your marker.

The plastic wrap seals the jar to keep water from evaporating.

3. Loosely seal the jar around the onion bulb and toothpicks with plastic cling wrap. Put a rubber band around the plastic wrap to hold it in place.

4. Put the onion in a sunny spot.

Roots will start growing after a few days!

5. Check your onion once a week. Measure the distance between your first water level mark and the new water level. Write down your results.

About how much water did your onion's roots take up each week?

Many desert plants have long roots. Their roots go deep to find water in dry soil.

Think It Through

As the roots grew, they took in water. They also took in minerals from the plant food that were dissolved in the water. Did you have a hot day? That made your onion take up more water.

Do Roots Always Grow Down?

Why don't plants get swept away by wind and rain? Their roots anchor them down. When a seed starts to grow, the first part that grows is the roots.

You may see a seedling's stem and leaves first. But roots are the first part of a seed to grow.

Which direction do the roots grow? An experiment will tell us.

What you need:

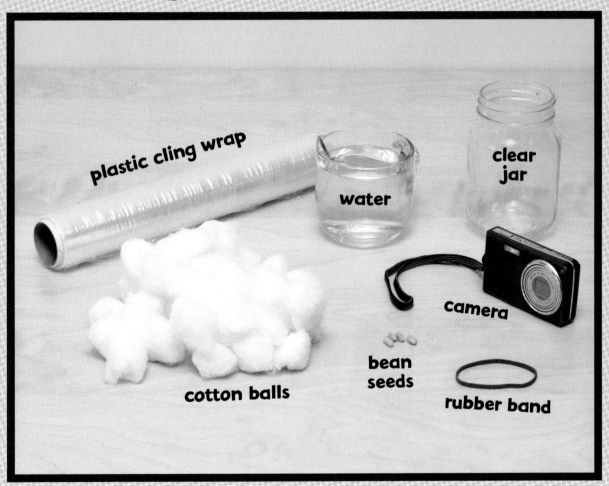

plastic cling wrap

water

clear jar

cotton balls

bean seeds

camera

rubber band

Steps:

1. Fill the jar with cotton balls.

2. Plant the bean seeds in the jar.

3. Add just enough water to the jar to get all the cotton balls wet.

Plant the seeds as close to the jar's walls as you can. That way you can see them.

4. Place plastic cling wrap on top of the jar. Put a rubber band around the wrap to hold it in place.

Take a picture of the roots every day. This will help you track how the roots are growing.

After about a week, roots will sprout! Let the roots grow for several days.

You've let the roots grow for a while.

5. Now try turning the jar over. Let the roots grow for several more days.

Think It Through

The roots changed direction! They kept growing down, even when you turned the jar upside down.

Roots grow down into the soil. This helps prevent soil from washing away during rainstorms.

Can a Piece of Carrot Root Grow New Leaves?

Roots take in minerals from the soil. They move the minerals up through the stem to other parts of the plant. These minerals help plants grow.

Minerals help plants make their own food using sunlight.

Some roots have an extra job. They are like a plant's kitchen cupboard. The roots store some of the food for the plant.

Sweet potatoes are tasty roots that store food for the rest of the plant.

Some plants, such as carrots, store lots of food. That's what makes a carrot's fat, orange root so good to eat. Let's see what happens when we put the food energy in a carrot to work.

Plants such as carrots store food we can eat.

What you need:

water

bowl

carrot with greens

knife

Steps:

1. With an adult's help, cut the carrot to a 1-inch (2.5-centimeter) piece.

2. Then, cut the greens down to 1 inch (2.5 cm).

Now let's get your carrot ready to grow!

Add enough water to cover the bottom of the carrot.

3. Put the cut carrot into the bowl.

4. Add water to the bowl.

Check your carrot every day. Soon it will grow new leaves!

Your carrot leaves sprouted without soil or plant food.

Think It Through

Your carrot leaves used the stored food in the carrot root to grow. Think of another plant that stores food in its roots, such as a radish. Predict what might happen if you tried the carrot experiment with the new plant. Experiment to find out if you were right!

Tasty radishes store food we can eat in their roots, just as carrots do.

Observe Like a Scientist

Looking carefully, or observing, is an important skill for a scientist. Here are some tips to help you be a good observer of plants:

1. Don't just look. Ask an adult to help you make sure a plant is safe to touch. If it is, touch and smell the plant.

2. Notice the plant's details.

3. Change your view. Try looking under the leaves.

Fun Facts

- Not all roots grow in soil. Some plant roots take up minerals as the plant floats through the water.

- Some plants grow on trees. They use their roots to cling to branches.

- Roots help create soil. As roots grow they crush underground rocks. These rock pieces later become soil.

- Mangrove tree roots prop the tree up in shallow ocean water.

Glossary

energy: the ability to make things move, light up, or do other work

mineral: a natural substance that comes from the earth and often helps living things survive

prediction: a good guess about what might happen in the future

record: to write something down so it can be saved

root: a plant part that takes in water and nutrients

stem: the main part of a plant that leaves and flowers grow from

Further Reading

Biology4kids: Plants
http://www.biology4kids.com/files/plants_structure.html

Burnie, David. *Plant.* **Eyewitness Plant series. New York: Dorling Kindersley, 2011.**

Latham, Donna. *Backyard Biology: Investigate Habitats Outside Your Door with 25 Projects.* **White River Junction, VT: Nomad Press, 2013.**

Missouri Botanical Garden: Biology of Plants
http://www.mbgnet.net/bioplants/main.html

My First Garden
http://urbanext.illinois.edu/firstgarden

Sterling, Kristin. *Exploring Roots.* **Minneapolis: Lerner Publications, 2012.**

Index

Photo Acknowledgments

The images in this book are used with the permission of: © Rick Orndorf, pp. 2, 7, 11, 12, 13, 14, 17, 18, 19, 20, 25, 26 (top), 26 (bottom); © LehaKoK/Shutterstock Images, p. 4; © Richard Griffin/Shutterstock Images, p. 5; © siambizkit/Shutterstock Images, p. 6; © Red Line Editorial, p. 9; © Spotmatik/Thinkstock, p. 10; © Anton Foltin/Shutterstock Images, p. 15; © Jupiterimages/Thinkstock, pp. 16, 27; © sarkao/Shutterstock Images, p. 21; © AlinaMD/Shutterstock Images, p. 22; © Seiya Kawamoto/Thinkstock, p. 23; © Thomas Northcut/Thinkstock, p. 24; © Ijansempoi/Shutterstock Images, p. 28; © showcake/Thinkstock, p. 30; © Cathy Yeulet/Thinkstock, p. 31.

Cover: © Rosemary Calvert/Photographer's Choice/Getty Images.

Main body text set in Johann Light 30/36.